Toot! Toot!
Have a happy Christmas!
Shyla

CLARA CLAUS

A poem written by

SHYLA

Illustrated by

LARRY PARKHURST

ShyBooks
A DIVISION OF D-VOB

Revised Edition

Text and Illustrations Copyright © 1997 by ShyBooks

Published by ShyBooks
P.O. Box 1417
Lake Stevens, WA 98258

Library of Congress Catalog Card Number
97-68367

Clara Claus written by Shyla, illustrated by Larry Parkhurst

Summary: Christmas appears to be ruined because of the weather. Clara's idea saves the day!

ISBN 0-9658599-0-8

Printed and bound in the United States

TOOT TOOT!

To *My Children*
Cozette
Christy
Cindy
Cheri
and George

I wish each thought could be a bird,
Of bright and glorious blue.
To sing a song of happiness,
The whole day long to you.
Circa 1920, Author Unknown

Santa was worried this Christmas,

No snow had fallen as yet.

The skies were extremely cloudy,

And the ground was very wet.

"What shall I do?" he asked Clara.

"To travel is impossible this night.

No full moon to guide me,

And no snow in which to light."

Clara put her knitting aside.

She said, "Gather the helpers together,

With everyone wearing his thinking cap,

We'll soon have a solution to the weather."

Santa said,
"Clara, that's a wonderful thought!

I'll call them in right now.

Put on a pot of hot chocolate,

Then we'll have our little pow-wow."

They all tip-toed in together,

Sadness showing on each face.

"Sit here around us," said Clara,

"Warm yourselves by the fireplace."

Santa said, "I've told them of our plight,

Now let's hear what each has to say.

We must hurry on with the meeting,

For I must be on my way."

Elenore Elf spoke up first,

"Let's put wheels on the sleigh!

Maybe Dancer and Prancer can pull it!"

Santa said, "No, can't be done that way."

"In the first place, we'd get lost,

The fog is very, very thick,

The reindeer couldn't climb the hills,

I'd get cold and probably sick."

Peter Pixie piped up next,

"Let's postpone Christmas a day or two."

Santa said, "Can't disappoint the children,

No! No! That will never do!"

"Don't postpone Christmas!"
Screeched Flossy,

Tears dripping down to her feet.

Emery Elf started howling,

While Pinky turned red as a beet!

Clara poured the hot chocolate,

Then stood with hands on hips.

"For a bunch of elves and fairies,

You've forgotten a lot of your tricks!"

"We'll ask Gilda Goose to lend a hand,

And pluck all the geese we can find.

Then put all the feathers into sacks,

Let's see what else comes to mind."

"Oh yes! We'll call on old North Wind,

To blow the clouds aside.

We'll toss the feathers into the air,

Santa! Are you ready to ride?"

"Why, Clara that's a wonderful plan!"

Santa said, kissing his dear wife.

The elves tossed the feathers into the air,

Oh, it was a glorious sight!

Santa took off with a Ho! Ho! Ho!

Feeling joyous as a lark.

The moon was bright and shining,

Now it wouldn't be so dark.

Clara took up her knitting again.

And with her glasses on her nose to see,

With a merry twinkle in her eye, she thought,

"They could never get along without me."

THE CAST

Santa Claus   **Clara Claus**

Fergus Fairy   **Gilda Goose**

Peter Pixie   **Emery Elf**   **Flossy Fairy**   **Elenore Elf**   **Pinky Pixie**

All images and names of the characters on this page are trademarked™ with the exception of the name Santa Claus.

FAIRY TALES

A "Let's Learn" Page

Tales of supernatural creatures are common all over the world. In America we have some different names for them. We generally call them fairies, elves or pixies. These names, of course, originally came from other cultures. Other nations have their own special names for these beings. In Great Britain these creatures are sometimes called brownies or silkies. They're called kolbolds in Germany, goblins in France and shees in Ireland just to name a few. People tend to refer to the helpers at the North Pole as elves; however, fairies, pixies and the rest are all basically the same .

Although these creatures are different in some ways, they do have a lot in common. There seems to be some good ones and some naughty ones. They all like to play tricks on humans. The good ones play cute, fun tricks and the naughty ones can get rather mean. They all have some magical powers and are able to become invisible to human beings. Since they are very shy, they are almost always invisible. They all like music and most like to dance the nights away. The one exception is the shees of Ireland. They love music but they absolutely do not like to dance. Like humans, fairies and the like, come in various sizes, shapes and colors. None of them get very tall but they all have pointed ears.

There are a few of these magical little creatures who are very helpful to humans. You have just read about a few of them. Flossy, Elenore, Peter, Emery, Fergus, Gilda and Pinky love human beings, especially the children, and would never play tricks on them. What an honor it is for them to work with Clara and Santa at the North pole!

From The Cast and all of us at ShyBooks:
Merry Christmas the whole year through!